FIGMENT OF A TAINTED HEART

S.D. MAYERS

To my loving wife, Pauletta, whose boundless love and encouragement are the foundation of my strength; to my sweet daughter, Shanta, whose light and inspiration fill my heart with joy; to my family, whose steadfast support and belief in me keep me grounded; and to my friends, whose camaraderie and understanding are my constant refuge.

A heartfelt thank you to my readers, whose thoughtful feedback and insightful comments drive me to improve and grow. Your engagement and support mean the world to me.

With deepest gratitude,

S.D. Mayers

Contents

Chapter One: The Mirror's Reflection

My head is heavy with thoughts, swirling with condemnation. You feel it too, don't you? As my mother used to say, I've met very few who could understand my ways. She was always fussing with me, telling me what to do.

I was never much for talking and seldom defended myself in an argument until that fateful day when Mama pushed too far.

"Slut, jezebel, deviant, lazy, bland, vacuous, craven, obtuse." These were a few of her most voiced opinions of me. I had to look up half of these words in the dictionary.

Yet, despite the insults, she always ended with how pretty I was and how my skin reminded her of beautiful honey. My guess is honey was her favorite condiment. The bite marks on my back would attest to that.

I often stood in front of the mirror, silently screaming. How could Mama do these things to me? Was I truly such a terrible person? Maybe she saw something in me that I couldn't. I'd stare into the mirror, wishing I could disappear from this place of despair.

The year is 1999. Baton Rouge, Louisiana, is an excellent place, people say. But my whole life was filled with terror. Admittedly, there were a few pleasant spots, like the visit to the Zoo or the Knock Knock Children's Museum. That brought some joy and solace.

At the zoo, I enjoyed the children's petting zoo the most with all the domesticated animals. I always got a chance to feed them. One time, when I was close to feeding a pony, Mama pushed the apple out of my hand. It didn't look like anyone saw her do it, either.

Mama and I lived near the railroad tracks, about a mile from a local junkyard and another mile from the town lake. We lived in a small town, poor to middle-class people. The town smelled like an old industrial factory at times.

Our house was old and run down. And the roof needed fixing. If it rained, it rained real hard, and the water would drip on my pillow. Seemed like the water would follow me wherever I went on the bed.

The foot, middle, or head. It didn't seem to matter.

And if it was sunny, well, the sun seemed to chase you, trying to burn you to death.

Lost in my thoughts as I usually am, Mama abruptly interrupted. "Dear child," she would say, "Why do you look in the mirror for so long? You are a very vain child." She would smile as she said this, and then her smile would turn to an evil look.

"Yes, Mama," I would reply meekly, or sometimes, "Yes, Ma'am." It was always better not to anger her. Mama was quick to anger, and there was no telling what she could do.

Despite Mama's harsh opinions, my

school counselor, Mr. Resler, often told me, "Celeste, you are exceptional, inside and out." His words were a rare solace, a glimmer of hope in my otherwise bleak existence.

Mr. Resler also substituted for my math and science teachers. He would always say things like, "A mind is a terrible thing to waste."

I think he got that from an '80s commercial.

But let's focus on Mama for now, for she is where this story truly begins.

Are you ready to hear more? This is not for the fainthearted. Mama hated how I looked, walked, talked, spoke, ate, slept, cried, laughed—just about everything. But I don't think it was her fault.

Perhaps that was what she hated most about me: I felt sorry for her and wondered if she could ever heal from whatever hurt her so badly.

Mama never talked about her Mama. I wonder if Mama was treated like she treated me. The good book does say to do to others as you would like them to do onto to you. Maybe Mama didn't want to be treated well.

People would say Mama was some witch. I couldn't tell for sure. I could hear the whispering in the market when we sometimes would shop.

We would walk to the market or take the bus since we have no car. Mama mostly preferred to walk since it would give her more opportunities to torment me.

One day in the market, a boy many years younger than me ran to me and whispered in my ear. He said yo, mama, an evil bitch. But I think he meant witch.

Sometimes, after one of her evil spells, I would cry in front of the mirror and imagine myself in beautiful Paris with Mama, all well-fixed up and happy. We would walk and sing French songs, and everyone would admire our beauty.

But this was just a dream, a figment of my imagination. After crying, I'd lay in bed and cry some more. It was healing for me and made me feel better.

On this particular day, after my usual bout of weeping, I noticed something I hadn't before. Mama was standing in the hallway of our one-story house, watching my every movement.

The house was old and run down, like I said earlier; we only had two bedrooms, and the floorboards were creaky. So when anyone walked, you could hear their every footstep.

Her eyes were vacant, almost as if she was looking through me rather than at me. I called her, but she said nothing. She just stared. Then, she came in and sat on my bed.

Okay, you little bitch, now play me a tune," Mama said.

I loved to make up songs and play them on the piano. I loved to listen to great pianists like Bill Evans, Nina Simone, Herbie Hancock, and James Booker.

But my favorite was Ray Charles by far. I'm getting away from the point, and Mama looks at me as she does, just before a slap in the face follows.

"Bitch, didn't you hear what I just said," Mama said, followed by a very hard slap to my face.

A tear immediately fell to my cheek. "Yes, Mama," I replied as I began to play the piano. I started to sing a sorrowful tune. "My eyes are weak and heat to fleet, dust or riches will I meet," I sang and sang.

This seemed to calm Mama, who was in a

peculiar mood. "Child, you don't have to clean this house. I was testing you. Plus, it would be best if you had some discipline now and again."

Out of nowhere, Mama turned to me and said: "Maybe we should go somewhere far away where everyone would adore us." I looked at Mama in confusion as she continued echoing all my dreams and thoughts. What was happening to me?

"There is no way I could know these things or read your mind," Mama said, cutting me off mid-sentence. "Mama, how is this happening?

"I'm scared."

"I raised you and am the closest thing to a

mother. But I am certainly not your Mama." She replied,

At this point, I began to move cautiously away. The only exit was the window, which was at least a nine-foot drop.

My only option was to get out of there. Mama looked different, more terrifying, which scared me nearly to death.

Her eyes and hair were wild, and her lips were foaming. I repeated myself, asking if she was okay, but she looked at me as if I were a stranger—as if I were a completely different person.

Terror gripped me, freezing me in place as she slowly approached from across the room. My heart sank with a strange, weighted bliss as she came closer.

It felt like a release from this world, a freedom I never knew. Life for me seemed destined to be short-lived but hopefully meaningful. I thought about the possibilities, wondering where I might have gone wrong. There must be a reason for this.

Mama was gonna murder me, no question about it. My heart raced like it was beating a thousand times a second. I had never felt such fear and was frozen in place.

If I die, will anyone remember me? Will the schoolkids even think of me? I'm sure the boy who said Mama was a bitch would remember me.

I held my chest tight and closed my eyes

so tight my eyelids hurt.

Then I noticed my hands were covered in blood. I couldn't explain why. Mama—or whoever this woman was—did not seem as gruesome now, lying immobile on the old wooden floor.

Tell me, what is the name of the thing that scares you the most? For me, it's myself.

By now, you must be wondering who this ill-fated character is, questioning herself, her mother, her life, and many other things as I looked over the body of this slumped figure whom I called Mama.

My thoughts began to race. What to do? How do you explain this apparent murder? Mama seemed so lifeless and defenseless, not the monstrous figure from moments ago.

Fear surged within as I contemplated whether I could be the monster and Mama, a mere victim. What have I done? I started to second-guess this reality and my sanity.

It was early evening, and the moon was full and bright, casting an eerie glow. There were no sounds—no birds, no insects, nothing. The urge to run became overwhelming, but leaving would make me the prime suspect.

Who was I fooling? Shit, I am the prime suspect. And it didn't matter if I left or stayed.

So, what should I do? What would you do? My heart wrenched with guilt, and a wild flutter consumed my chest. I began to breathe heavily, feeling like there wasn't enough air.

What is happening to me? I had few choices. Should I stay and try to calm down or run like a thief in the night?

A moan came from deep inside my throat, almost feral. Am I a predator or just prey to an incipient calamity? What more could go wrong?

Is this the beginning or the end for me? My moan grew stronger, flowing from my stomach to my throat. I could barely contain it, my hands tightly grasping my mouth. Maybe I'm just hungry. But who could eat at a time like this?

Thoughts raced, and my memories were

so confused. Close your eyes and click your heels three times. It's like that old movie with the little girl and her dog. Mama loved that movie.

If I do this, my nightmare will disappear. It will vanish as though none of this occurred. Okay, here goes. I click my shoes and wish for home, wherever that is. But wait, if this is a dream, then what is real?

Whatever this is, clicking my feet in hopes of leaving this terrible nightmare is worth it. I'll try anything. SHIT, it didn't work!

Chapter Two: Aftermath

I stood there, frozen. Mama was dead. I had to move and think.

Finally, I forced myself to step away, my body moving awkwardly away from this horrible scene.

What I did to Mama was gonna cost me dearly. They might even give me the death penalty. Stupid, stupid, stupid. I hit my head in frustration.

Why the fuck did I kill that woman? I don't even know how I killed her.

I know one thing. I have to leave the body. I grabbed food: an apple, some bread, cheese, and a banana. Then I grabbed my school bag, clothes, and wallet.

There was just $2.35, enough for two

trips on the bus.

When I stepped outside, the air was refreshing, especially for a summer night. The only person that could help me now was Mr. Resler.

Mr. Resler had always been kind to me. I know what you're thinking. He was a molester. But this was not the case with Mr. Resler.

He stopped by my house once to drop off schoolwork when I was sick. Well, I wasn't sick. Mama had beat me almost to death, it felt.

And she didn't want me going to school with all the bruises showing. The bruises had healed by the time Mr. Resler came by. But he was uneasy in my house.

I guess that's because when Mama answered the door, she took a fancy to him and put her hands down his pants. You know where his manhood is.

Anyway, they didn't know, but I saw everything. Well, I take that back; Mama probably knew since she could read my mind and all.

After reviewing some challenging topics, Mr. Resler wrote down his home address in my notebook in case I needed somewhere safe.

Mr. Resler was friendly but seemed guarded. I was surprised that he even gave me his address.

I remember one of the girls saying he lost his wife and baby while she was in labor. I heard he didn't take it well. But that was a long time ago before I even came to High School.

Since he lost his wife and baby I hear Mr. Resler's main focus is on his students and the sciences.

I wonder if he has a girlfriend. Not that I would want to be his girlfriend—that would be disgusting—but maybe someone his age.

Looking back on these events, I realize he was a good man. Mr. Resler was the man you would want to be your dad. I was sad he lost his wife and unborn child.

I was cautious in the late-night hour. It was very dark. And some of the street lights were out, which made it even harder to see.

The ride on the bus was hazy, as I just kept reliving what had happened with Mama and all. My reflection in the bus mirror seemed weird, but I thought nothing of it then.

I thought Mama was not my Mama. She was some monster that I had somehow destroyed. Some supernatural being that knew my every thought.

Where did she come from? Did she steal me from my real Mama?

I wondered what else did Mama know if she read my thoughts. She must have known everything I thought of her. She must have hated me because I hated her. I hated her for her hateful words.

I hated her for the bites she put on my

back. I hated her for the beatings she —.

I cried just thinking of all this, weeping while trying not to be noticed by strangers.

The bus wasn't that crowded since it was late. From what I remember, it was maybe four or five people. But it's hazy of what they looked like.

I was too busy in my mess to concentrate on them.

When I finally reached Mr. Resler's neighborhood, it was almost midnight. The quiet suburban streets were just about empty. The street lights were in better condition as Mr. Resler lived in a better neighborhood than me.

I was scared walking through Mr.

Resler's neighborhood. Although his neighborhood seemed safe. I was still cautious.

Mr. Resler's house was a modest, one-story single-family home. The porch light was still on. My hand shook as I rang the doorbell.

I thought, Mr. Resler must have a good amount of scratch leaving his light on all night. By scratch, I mean money.

After what felt like forever, the door opened.

"Celeste?" Mr. Resler opened the door wearing plaid dad pajamas; his voice tone was a concerning one. Oh, I wished right then, and there he was, my daddy.

Mr. Resler was a thin man in his mid-30s, with kind eyes behind wire-rimmed glasses and a gentle demeanor. "What are you doing here?"

"I didn't know where else to go," I stammered. "Something terrible has happened."

He ushered me inside, his eyes wide with worry. "Sit down, tell me what happened."

As I explained everything to Mr. Resler, his face turned from concern to disbelief. I feel like he was disappointed with me.

But why would he be disappointed? Had he not heard the horrifying events I so carefully laid out?

"Celeste, You killed your mother. This is a very serious thing. It would be best if you went to the police." he said when I finished.

Shit, I thought Mr. Resler didn't trust me anymore. For all I know, he might think I could kill him, too.

"No!" I almost shouted. "They'll think I did it. You don't understand, Mr. Resler. She wasn't my mother, not really. She knew things she shouldn't have. She was reading my mind. I don't think Mama was human."

He looked at me for a long moment, then nodded slowly. "If you don't go to the police, I will call them right now." Mr. Resler said.

I began to cry and fell to the ground. It felt like my mind was crashing. I started to hit my head with my hand while sobbing uncontrollably.

Mr. Restler rushed over to me and held my hands, picking me up gently.

"Okay, okay. We'll figure this out. But you can't stay here. It's not safe."

"Where can I go?" I asked, panic rising again.

What did Mr. Resler have planned for me? Did he believe me or think of me as a lunatic?

"I have a friend, an old colleague. She runs a shelter for women in crisis. I'll call her. She'll help you."

I found this odd; Mr. Resler quickly

found someone this time of night who could help me, but I had no other choice.

I nodded, too exhausted to argue. Mr. Resler picked up the phone and made the call, speaking in low, urgent tones.

I looked over Mr. Resler, as he looked concerned while talking to this woman who would supposedly come to my rescue at this hour at night.

After a few minutes, he hung up.

"She'll meet you at the bus station in an hour. Her name is Claudine. She's expecting you."

"Thank you," I whispered, tears of relief welling up.

He hugged me tightly. "We'll get to the bottom of this, I promise."

But, I was still concerned and weary of why Mr.Resler would let a 16-year-old girl walk by herself to a bus station in the middle of the night.

I know it's not just me. Don't you find this strange? What is Mr. Resler up to?

I trusted him, but now I'm second-guessing my view of this man. But I had to continue to my destination.

The bus station was nearly empty at this hour. The dim lighting cast long shadows, making everything seem more ominous.

That's a word Mama would use to

describe a sinister situation.

I sat on a bench, trying to stay calm. Every rustle of leaves or distant sound made my heart race. When a woman approached, I knew it had to be Mr. Resler's friend.

She was a short woman in her late 30s, with a kind face framed by curly hair and a kind face. Though filled with concern, her eyes had a spark of determination that made me feel slightly safer.

"Celeste?" she asked softly.

I nodded. "Yes."

"Come with me. I'm Ms. Claudine," she said, extending a hand. "You're safe now."

I followed her to a car parked nearby, my mind racing but my heart slightly lighter.

As we drove through the quiet streets, my mind was calmer, but I felt uneasy still. Could I trust Ms. Claudine?

The drive to the shelter was silent, except for the occasional engine hum. Ms. Claudine kept glancing at me, her eyes filled with concern, but she didn't press for details.

When we arrived at the shelter, a modest two-story brick building in the city area of town, Ms. Claudine led me inside.

It was nice. But anywhere would appear friendly after leaving the woman who called herself my

Mama.

I think that's what I'll call her because there's no chance in hell that woman was my mother.

Ms. Claudine showed me to a small room with a bed and dresser. The view was the side of another brick building.

But I didn't care. Shoot, I was too tired to care.

"This is your room," Ms. Claudine said gently. "You can stay here as long as you need. We'll talk more in the morning, okay?"

"Thank you," I whispered, my voice barely audible. Exhaustion weighed heavily on me, and I collapsed onto the bed, falling into a fitful sleep.

That night, I had strange dreams about Mama and everything that had happened. Mama grabbed me while I tried to escape and biting me on the back.

I couldn't get away from her no matter how fast I ran; she would keep biting the flesh off of my back.

Mama did things like this, but in the dream, the events were out of place. They were in public settings, and no one acted like anything was happening.

Mama would never do something like this in public. Instead, she would do things like this while we were home. If we were in public, her physical and mental abuse was more subtle.

Morning came too soon. Sunlight streamed through the window, waking me from a restless sleep. For a moment, I forgot where I was.

You know what I mean when you first awake and are not coherent enough to grasp the current history of events.

In the past, this would happen when I awoke and thought Mama wasn't so bad. But then the memories would always come back.

And the memories of the previous night did indeed come flooding back. I sat up, trying to steady my breathing.

A soft knock on the door interrupted my thoughts. "Celeste? It's Ms. Claudine. Can I come in?"

"Sure," I replied, my voice shaky.

She entered, carrying a tray with breakfast—toast, scrambled eggs, and a steaming cup of tea. "I thought you might be hungry," she said, setting the tray on the small table by the window.

"Thanks," I said, though I didn't feel much like eating.

I would later regret this choice of not eating such a delicious meal.

Ms. Claudine sat down across from me, her expression severe but kind. "I know you've been through a lot, Celeste. Whenever you're ready, I'm here to listen."

"Are you here to listen?" I thought to

myself. I wondered if she was a version of Mama. She seemed different, but I didn't know if I could trust her.

"Celeste, are you okay?" Ms. Claudine said.

I nodded, taking a sip of tea. The warmth was comforting, and it gave me the courage to speak.

"It's a long story," I began. "I don't even know where to start."

"Start wherever you feel comfortable," she encouraged.

But where should I have started? Should I start from a child and relay all the cruel things Mama did to me? Or should I start tonight?

After breathing deeply, I recounted the events that had led me here—my tumultuous relationship with Mama, the terrifying encounter that ended with her lifeless body, and my desperate flight to Mr. Resler's house.

Ms. Claudine listened intently, her expression never wavering.

When I finished, she reached out and gently squeezed my hand. "You've been courageous, Celeste. What you went through is unimaginable. But you're safe here, and we'll do everything we can to help you."

"Do you think I'm crazy?" I asked, my voice barely a whisper.

"No," she said. "You're not crazy.

Ms. Claudine assured me she had my back. But did she?

I nodded, still unsure what to think of Ms. Claudine or Mr. Resler.

Why didn't they call the police? Maybe the police were coming, and Ms. Claudine was stalling me.

If they didn't call the police, then did they check my house for Mama's body? I would think that's something they would want to do right away.

Mr. Resler, that's why he was acting funny. He probably wanted to get over there quickly and verify everything I said. Mama being dead and all.

Chapter Three: On the Run

The sun had set, casting long shadows across the shelter's garden as Ms. Claudine sat in her small office.

I imagine she had encountered many women at the shelter, each with complex issues. However, my story involved a murder, and this came with another level of fear and concern.

I knew I was a liability to her.

I could see the concern in Ms. Claudine's eyes.

I had arrived in a state of shock, my eyes wide with terror. I believed I had killed my mother, but my accounts were filled with paranoia and delusion.

I know now she was waiting for some

confirmation from Mr. Resler that Mama was dead or

alive. I feel in my heart Mama is dead. But what if I'm

wrong and she's alive? And I just left her there. Did she

deserve to die?

She glanced at the clock. It was nearly

time for dinner. With a deep sigh, she left her office and

walked towards the common area where Mr. Resler was

waiting.

I watched her leave through a crack in the

door, my heart pounding. I had been hiding in the

shadows, listening to every word they said. I knew what

they were up to and planned to involve the police.

I couldn't let that happen—a slight moan

from within rose. I prayed no one heard as I continued to

listen.

"Claudine," Mr. Resler greeted her. He looked worried. "How is she?"

"Scared and confused," Claudine replied, rubbing her temples. "I don't know what to do. She needs help, but I'm torn about involving the police. What if she did something terrible?"

Mr. Resler nodded, understanding her dilemma. "We have to consider her mental state. She's distressed and may not fully understand what's happening."

They walked together towards the dining room, where I hurried back and sat alone at a corner table, picking at my food and pretending to eat.

My eyes darted around the room, and Ms. Claudine saw I was nervous. She approached slowly, not wanting to startle me.

"Hey, Celeste," Ms. Claudine said softly, sitting across from me. "How are you feeling?"

I shrugged, not meeting her gaze. I started to think of when I was a little girl and all the cruel things Mama did to me.

I remember my first memory of Mama. She wasn't smiling. She seemed angry and full of hate. I don't know how old I was, but she was looking down on me, so I must have been very young.

Could I have been? A baby? No, that couldn't be possible.

I'm sorry I got sidetracked again. Let me continue. I'll try my best and focus on my story without too many interruptions.

I looked at Ms. Claudine, trying to think of a response to her question. How does she expect me to feel, I thought?

This may be part of her intake process, and she is trying to figure me out. I don't trust her completely, but she doesn't seem evil like Mama.

"I don't know. Everything's so confusing." I replied. I had a slight headache, as I get from time to time. Sometimes, they can be terrible migraines, but this was not too bad, just annoying.

Ms. Claudine nodded, her heart aching

for me. "It's okay to feel that way. You've been through a lot. But I want you to know that you're safe here. We're here to help you."

I looked up, eyes searching Ms. Claudine's face for any sign of deceit. "Are you going to call the police?"

Ms. Claudine's heart skipped a beat. I knew she had been dreading this question. I looked closer to see her response.

I could feel her pulse as I stretched out and reached her wrist. It was rising, and I knew she was a liar. I held her wrist firmly. Maybe a little too firm

"Let go! You're hurting me," Ms. Claudine said.

I was shocked she was hurt and let go.

Ms Claudine rubbed her wrist, "Celeste, right now, my priority is helping you. We're just trying to figure out the best way to do that.

"You're a LIAR! I said abruptly. I pushed my plate away and stood up abruptly. "I don't trust you," I muttered before hurrying out of the dining room.

Later that evening, maybe around 10 pm, I found a hiding spot near the office where I could overhear Ms. Claudine and Mr. Resler discussing their options.

I decided to sit in the lounge area. Ms. Claudine's office area was close by, and Mr. Resler had just entered in a flurry.

I ran to the door just as Mr. Resler slammed it shut. Luckily, most people were in the dining area, so no one noticed me. As I listened, I could hear their muffled voices.

"She's so fragile right now," Ms. Claudine said, her voice breaking.

"I know Claudine, and to make things even more complicated, Celeste's mother was murdered. The last person to see her was Celeste.

"Do you think she could hurt another person?" Ms. Claudine said.

Mr. Resler paused. "I'm not sure, but we can't take any chances, Claudine."

"We must turn Celeste in soon; the police

are crawling all over her home. And if we don't, we will certainly be accessories to this crime," Mr. Resler said.

"No, we can't just yet. She's just a child. Can't she stay just for tonight?" Ms. Claudine said.

"If we involve the police now, God knows what will happen to Celeste. Don't you remember what they did to my cousin?" Ms. Claudine said.

"They raped and hung her while in custody. And claimed she killed herself. We all know that child would have never done that to herself." Ms. Claudine said.

"You remember their only punishment was suspension. Pierre, I'm scared for this child." Ms.

Claudine said.

I could hear Ms. Claudine crying after recounting what happened to her cousin.

Then it got really quiet for a few minutes. I wonder if Mr. Resler and Ms. Claudine were fooling around.

Let's explain everything to Celeste in the morning, and we can all go to the police station." Mr. Resler said.

"Okay, maybe I was overreacting. And we may have a shot for her freedom once the court sees Celeste's psychological condition." Ms. Claudine said.

"That's my girl." Mr. Resler said.

As night fell, the shelter grew quiet. Ms. Claudine looked upset. She checked on me one last time before turning in for the night.

She knocked softly on the door to my room but received no answer. Cautiously, she opened the door and found the room empty.

Ms. Claudine panicked. "Celeste?" she called out, hoping for a response. She quickly checked the bathroom and the common areas, but I was nowhere to be found.

I was not going to turn myself in to the police. I'm a young black girl, and they are not gonna believe anything I say.

I ain't got no money or any resources to

pay for a good attorney either. Oh my God, they're

gonna lock me up forever.

That's what happened to poor Zachariah.

He was 18 and came back home from college to visit

everybody. Anyways, Zachariah decided to teach his

little brother Sam how to swim out at the lake.

I guess Sam didn't catch on quickly

enough. Sam was just nine when he drowned to death,

and they gave Zachariah life in prison.

Someone testified that they thought it was

premeditated on account they publicly disagreed all the

time.

But I knew Zachariah and Sam. They

mostly had fun debating one another. You see,

Zachariah was studying prelaw, and Sam wanted to be just like his big brother.

So that's what they did. But people would give them strange looks from time to time.

I can see the judge throwing the book at me literally. And my half-assed attorney is looking pitifully at me and saying how sorry they were. And that maybe we could get an appeal.

Mr. Resler and Ms. Claudine would also be sitting in there looking dumb as rocks because they sent an innocent child to prison or, worse, the death penalty.

Oh hell to the naw, they ain't killing me. I needed to leave quickly and unseen.

To Ms. Claudine's knowledge, I had run away. I would eventually run away but stayed hidden, watching her.

Ms. Claudine sat down on the edge of the bed, her head in her hands. She wept, and I wondered if I had been mistaken about her.

I understand she and Mr. Resler were trying to help me. But it didn't make sense how they were going about it.

And not to mention, Mr. Resler is an intelligent man, and I'm sure he saw signs of abuse, like the bite marks on my back. I remember one time he did ask about it.

I stupidly made up a story that the

neighborhood dog bit me.

But everybody knows that old Satchel wouldn't hurt a soul. I loved that old dog. I named him Satchel after the negro leagues legend Satchel Paige.

Old Satchel, I'm talking about the dog now, was bright and could still do a lot of tricks, like rolling over and playing dead.

Old Satchel was very intelligent, just like the baseball player Satchel Page. He was especially good at playing dead until one day when I went to see him. He was dead for real.

I'm getting sidetracked again. My point is, Mr. Resler must have known, so why would they turn me in? Let me get back to Ms. Claudine.

I continued to watch Ms. Claudine as she prayed. It wasn't easy to hear her because she was speaking so softly. But despite her voice being very quiet, I did manage to listen to some of what Ms. Claudine said.

"Please be safe, Celeste," Ms. Claudine whispered. "Please come back." Outside, the city was quiet as I ran through the streets, tears streaming down my face.

I felt betrayed now that I knew for sure Ms. Claudine and Mr. Resler would turn me over to the police.

I finally left undetected, thoughts racing; I started second-guessing myself as I cautiously walked through downtown Baton Rouge. Maybe, Ms. Claudine and Mr Resler, suspected I was up to something...

How could anyone not think that I was deranged? My head was pounding, and that all-too-familiar moan resounded from within my belly.

I felt lost, not knowing how to turn, but some kind of instinct drove me forward. After what seemed like forever, I stumbled into a narrow, dimly lit alley.

I was so drained and just slumped against a peeling brick wall, tears streaming down my face, my sobs breaking the eerie silence of the night.

I danced in the night to calm myself. Did I ever tell you that I could dance? You know, elegant like a ballet dancer.

I had no formal training but watched how peaceful and graceful those dancers were. And it did bring me peace, just like playing the piano and singing.

As I danced, my legs moved awkwardly as I tried to focus on the dance and not the woman who called herself my Mama.

But it didn't help this time. I was too sad to dance.

"Why is this happening to me?" I cried into the night, my voice echoing off the empty buildings.

I covered my mouth, startled by how loud it was and afraid I would be discovered. I pulled my knees to my chest and rocked back and forth, trying to calm the storm inside my mind.

After a while, I lay on the cold, hard ground. The alley offered little comfort, but it was my only; this was all I had right now. This was all I had.

"My eyes are weak and heat to fleet, dust or riches will I meet," I sang softly, hoping no one could hear as I slowly fell into a sleep.

Chapter Four: The Fractured Reality

I didn't sleep well that night in the elements, vulnerable to God knows what. I dreamt of my last encounter with Mama as she tried to kill me, and I barely escaped with my life.

She must have been a supernatural being or a demon. How else could she have read my mind? The oddness of this whole situation disgusted me.

The dream continued to another scenario: when I was just a little girl, Mama would put me outside for hours and delight in the event of unbearable weather like rain or if it was extreme heat.

She seemed annoyed if the day turned out to be moderately hot. In this dream, I somehow escaped Mama.

I awoke with tears in my eyes and weak, not just physically but emotionally. The smell of rotting garbage and the sound of distant traffic made me sick to the stomach.

I was lying in a filthy alley, my body covered in trash. For a moment, I was disoriented, struggling to remember where I was and how I had gotten here.

The previous night's events came rushing back, and a wave of fear and confusion washed over me. I looked to the edge of the dumpster and noticed a set of bricks lying out of place.

I remember the time when Mama hit me with a brick one day. She told the doctor I fell. I'm surprised I didn't die. Sorry, I'm getting away from the story again.

But one more thing: Mama was happy that I cried when it rained or was too sunny. I cried more than I needed to because I knew she would leave me be.

But I'm getting away from the story, as I sometimes will. I'm sorry. I'll continue and try my best not to go off track.

The following day, the sun's warmth hit my face, and my eyes were still closed; I couldn't believe what had happened to me.

A puddle of water was nearby, and though I was very thirsty, I resisted the urge to drink. The water was not safe to drink, and I could get sick and, who knows, maybe die.

As I looked at the puddle, my reflection changed. And then it changed again very slightly while I was looking.

The person in the reflection was not me, as I remembered. What the fuck is happening to me? Am I crazy? Is this person in the mirror me?

I observed closer, and my features were sharper, more distinct, but somehow recognizable. But this is not me, I thought.

People were around but not nearby; however, I heard something or someone approaching from a distance. I would have to figure this out later.

As I sat up, brushing off bits of refuse, I

noticed a figure approaching me from the mouth of the alley. My heart began to race. As it drew closer, the figure raised its hands in a gesture of peace.

It was Mr. Resler.

"Celeste, it's me," he called out gently. "I've been looking for you."

My mind raced. How had he found me? I felt a surge of panic and anger. "Stay away from me! I know what you're up to." I shouted, as my voice trembled.

Mr. Resler must be a supernatural being or something to have found me so quickly. A small groan came from within my belly.

Mr. Resler stopped a few feet away, his

hands still raised. "Celeste, please. I'm here to help you. We need to talk about what happened. You need to turn yourself in."

The mention of turning myself in ignited a fury within me. "You don't understand!" I screamed. "Mama wasn't human! She was a supernatural being, and now you're here trying to trick me!"

Mr. Resler looked both concerned and frustrated. "Celeste, listen to yourself. There are no supernatural beings. You're confused. You need help."

His words only made me angrier.

"No! You're lying! You're one of them, aren't you? You're trying to deceive me; I know it, for this is the truth now!"

At this point, my voice was up and down in pitch, and I could hardly believe I was speaking.

"You knew what she was, and you left me there to be abused. You're a smart man, and I know you knew!"

Mr. Resler took a cautious step forward. "Celeste, you need to calm down. I'm not here to hurt you. Please, let me help."

"Don't you come any closer, Mr. Resler," I said, my tone even more unfamiliar. "Something is going on here that I can't explain. Do you recognize me?
"

Mr. Resler paused and looked now only a few feet away.

"Celeste, you look somehow a little different. It's most likely just due to stress. But that's not the point; we can sort through that later," Mr. Resler replied.

Now, I knew this was confirmation that something dastardly was afoot. Mr. Resler continued to move closer. But his approach only made me more enraged.

"How the fuck could this be stress? I look very different. There are things not right here. Why would you want to turn me in to the police knowing I was abused?"

"Get away from me!" I shrieked, backing up against the wall. My eyes darted around for an escape route, but there was none.

Seeing no other option, Mr. Resler reached out, trying to take my hand. "Celeste, come with me. We'll get through this together."

In a blind panic, I shoved him away with all my strength.

Mr. Resler stumbled backward and tripped on the bricks I had noticed earlier.

He fell, his head striking the edge of a metal dumpster. I heard his neck snap and a cracking sound that must have been his skull.

Time seemed to freeze as I watched in horror. Mr. Resler lay motionless, his neck twisted at an unnatural angle. Blood pooled beneath his head, soaking into the dirt and grime of the alley.

A horrible silence descended, but I could still hear a distant hum of the city. I was trembling. At first, my mind struggled to process what had happened.

The blood from the back of Mr. Resler's skull soaked the concrete flowing towards my shoe. I backed away slowly, holding my breath until a scream creeped out.

I looked frantically at all sides of the alley, but no one seemed to hear me.

I couldn't understand how he could die so quickly. I pushed him. But I'm a sixteen-year-old girl, and he's a man.

Slowly, my terror began to subside, and I

began to see what was really going on.

This was proof, evidence that the world was filled with supernatural beings hunting me. I had been right all along.

I began to panic. I had to think of a plan, a way to leave this city of Baton Rouge. Being deep in the French Quarter near Cabido Alley, which extended from Pirate's Alley to St. Peter Street, was a good thing.

The Amtrak station wasn't too far away, maybe a little over a mile.

I could sneak onto the train undetected.

Anywhere would be better than Baton Rouge. But this wouldn't work. They check your tickets.

And I would stick out like a sore thumb.

A mangy-looking black girl. The first thing the conductor would ask is, "Ticket, please," followed by a bunch of other questions.

Shit, before long, I would be found out and sent to police custody.

I had to play devil's advocate like Zachariah used to say.

Did I kill Mr. Resler, the supernatural being? Or am I just deranged?

Deep down, I wondered if something was seriously wrong. I had just killed Mr. Resler, a man who had tried to help me.

I couldn't afford to dwell on it. I had to keep moving to stay ahead of the supernatural beings closing in on me.

I looked at Mr. Resler's lifeless body for the last time and fled the alley. I walked through the streets for hours, my mind swirling with fear and confusion.

Tears streamed down my face as I sobbed uncontrollably. The night was coming again, and I hadn't eaten.

But I couldn't risk being seen. Would anyone notice me, I thought. As I passed local shops, I noticed my reflection, and my face changed considerably.

God help me. I'm either crazy, or something terrible had happened to me to cause this change. Is this a shift in my reality, my appearance, or both?

It was a fact Mr. Resler mentioned I didn't look the same. Now, I was unsure if he acknowledged my face had physically changed or that I looked physically and emotionally distraught.

Oh, why didn't I clarify this with him?

I reacted too quickly, and Mr. Resler could have helped me sort out my version of reality, even if he was a supernatural being.

Maybe he was still in some way looking out for me.

Why did I have to push Mr. Resler to his death? Shit, if my face were changing, it wouldn't have mattered. Jesus, I killed Mr. Resler for nothing! God, please forgive me.

Eventually, I found myself in another desolate alley, far from the murder scene. I've committed two murders in the same week. God help me.

Exhausted and emotionally drained, I collapsed against a wall, my body drenched with sweat. The alley was quiet, offering a temporary refuge from my torment.

As I curled up on the cold ground, I whispered to myself, trying to make sense of the madness. "They're real. They have to be. I'm not crazy.

I'm not..."

"Hey, move you in my spot, gal!" Said a bum. I was startled because I had just fallen asleep and hadn't noticed this man.

I obliged and moved to another area. But it was hard to sleep now, knowing I was not alone in these alleys. I would have to be careful going forward.

Chapter Five: Days Gone

I awoke the following day. This is day 4, to my estimation, but I could be wrong.

My body ached from sleeping on the cold, hard ground, and my mind was a little hazy.

The previous day's events played out like a nightmare. Mr. Resler's lifeless body, the blood, the sound of his neck breaking—it all felt unreal, yet painfully vivid.

Was Mr. Resler a dead human or a dead supernatural being? If he was a dead supernatural being, then I could better deal with that.

But if he was a human, then God forgive me. I

killed an innocent man. I don't know what to think anymore. Did Mr. Resler have a relationship with Mama and Ms. Claudine?

I don't know that either. But I do know, Mama was real friendly. She ain't never been that friendly with nobody.

And Ms. Claudine was in a closed room with him for at least 5 minutes.

The boys at school would say it took less time than that to get their business done.

So, it is possible that Mr. Ressler had relations

with both Mama and Ms. Claudine. If he had relations

with Mama, he had to be something other than human.

Oh God, Mr. Resler and Mama! The thought

made me cringe.

And I don't care how crazy this sounds; I know

for sure the woman who called herself my Mama was no

human. So who's to say there weren't more creatures

like her in our town?

Mr. Resler being one of them.

There's another thing that keeps buggin' me.

Why didn't Mr. Resler just come with the police to come

get me in the alley? Why was it so important that he escorted me to the authorities?

I don't get that shit at all.

Nobody came to escort Zachariah to the police. The police came and got his ass.

There was also the terrible possibility that something was indeed happening to me or that I was indeed insane.

There was a puddle nearby, and I looked to see if my reflection was the same or had changed. But my face wasn't visible enough to tell if there had been any changes.

I could only feel my face for any changes, but it felt the same as it always did as a child.

The sun was shining mighty bright, just like it would back in my old rickety house.

I had no idea where I was or where to go next. I knew this was Lousianna, but it looked different—like a completely different town.

As I thought about this some more, I realized the city was more active with people, and there seemed to be more buses running.

The city felt unfamiliar. I needed to continue to keep a low profile if I was to survive. But I also needed to know where I was.

My stomach growled, a reminder that I hadn't eaten since the day before. I had no money, and I was alone and desperate.

I stumbled out of the alley, eyes scanning the streets for any sign of danger. The city was waking up, and people were starting their day.

However, as I said earlier, many more people were still on the street, especially for this time of day.

* * *

But nobody seemed to pay me no mind.

I moved quickly, trying to avoid eye contact with anyone who passed by.

Wandering through the streets, my mind a whirlwind of thoughts. I needed help, but who could I trust?

Mr. Resler was gone, and Ms. Claudine would surely turn me in to the police.

I do regret not eating the breakfast Ms. Claudine offered—toast, scrambled eggs, and a steaming cup of tea. It smelled so good.

But I turned it down, along with other food. So busy spying on everybody, I hardly ate anything.

Every face, although they were strangers, was a constant reminder that I was now alone in this world. My stomach growled even more now.

This city looked so different. As my stomach growled, I felt something was wrong with the landscape. There were tall skyscrapers.

And I had never seen so many in one city.

* * *

I had never been this hungry before; even Mama would feed me out of fear of people finding out she abused me. I think, especially after she hit me in the head with a brick, she was scared I would tell someone what happened.

Hours passed, and my hunger continued to grow even more unbearable. I found myself outside a small bakery.

It read.

RACQUEL'S BAKERY

ALWAYS FRESH AND ALWAYS YUMMY!

* * *

COME INSIDE AND TRY ONE OF OUR

DELICIOUS BAGELS!

The aroma of fresh food was intoxicating. The sign did say to come inside and try a delicious bagel.

I bet it is delicious.

I gotta eat, but what if someone recognized me? What if they called the police?

My heart was pounding, but I decided to take a leap of faith. I pulled the hood of my jacket up, covered my face as best as I could, and slipped inside.

* * *

This was probably not the best thing to do since everyone was now looking at the hooded black girl suspiciously.

I tried my best to ignore the strange glances and slowly put the hood jacket down.

Argh! Why did I even do that? I gotta think things through more.

The store was small, the aisles cramped with shelves of bakery items. They even had one of those food heaters with an assortment of premade breakfast sandwiches.

* * *

I moved quickly and grabbed a sausage egg and cheese bagel to slip into my pocket. But the cashier was eyeing me like a hawk, so I just started walking towards the counter.

As I reached the counter, the cashier, a middle-aged woman with kind eyes, smiled at me. "Good morning. Just these?"

I nodded, my voice catching in my throat. "Yes, thank you."

The woman rang up the items, her smile never wavering. "That'll be $5.75."

* * *

This may not seem like a lot of money, but for me, it seemed impossible to obtain. I was okay at pickpocket people's pockets.

But it was dangerous, and I didn't want to draw unnecessary attention. Plus, people didn't seem to carry cash like they used to.

I would need to go to the shelter, but my gut seemed to always keep me away from places like that.

My heart sank. I had no money. Panic surged through me, but I forced myself to stay calm and managed to whisper barely. "I... I don't have any money,

I'm sorry."

The woman's smile faded, replaced by a look of concern. "Are you okay, dear? You look like you've been through a lot."

I felt tears welling up in my eyes. "Please, I just need some food. I'm sorry."

My stomach growled in agreement. And I know she heard it because she looked down at my stomach for an instant before her attention refocused on my face.

The cashier studied me for a moment, then nodded. "It's okay. Please take it. Just promise me you'll be careful out there."

I was not okay and desperately in need of food. More than what she was offering. But it would have to be enough. I would have to make it work.

I nodded, too choked up to speak. Hardly managing the words, I said, "Thank you." Then I asked, "Can you tell me what city this is?"

With a concerned look and tone, the cashier responded, "Sweetheart, this is Chicago."

Almost stumbling in disbelief, I could hardly believe what she had said, but I needed to know for sure if I was truly mad. Finding composure, I asked, "What year is it?"

As the cashier looked at me with deep concern, she stepped from behind the counter and said, "Baby, the year is 2000. Are you okay?"

I gasped in disbelief, trying to understand because, in my mind, it was 1999, just a few days ago. That means I'm 17 years old now.

But how is this possible? I looked at the cashier, now staring fiercely. I had to maintain my composure, at least until leaving her sight.

* * *

If not, she would surely call the police.

"I'm sorry, I'm a little lightheaded from not eating." I said with a forced, reassuring look.

The cashier looked me over as her expression changed to a lighter demeanor. "Ok, sweaty, just be careful out there. There is a local shelter not too far from here. Please seek their assistance. And take care, okay." She said.

"Yes, ma'am," I replied. Then I grabbed the food and fled the store, my heart pounding with relief and guilt. I continued to walk and eat, searching this new city for a shelter the woman clerk had mentioned.

* * *

As the day wore on, I continued to wander, my mind trapped in a relentless cycle of fear and confusion. Is it possible I've lived on the streets for a year? Not to mention, I somehow managed to make it to Chicago.

I am truly mad and cannot trust myself if this is true. My reality is not reality at all. There are no supernatural beings!

But is this a trick of some manner? Could I be under some spell? I can't rule that out, either. At least I'm away from Mama.

At least she is gone for good and can't hurt me

anymore.

I passed the shelter but was too afraid to go in. The streets may be safer, at least for tonight. I'll think about it tomorrow. But as I said before, my gut has always told me not to go into shelters under any circumstances.

My thoughts flooded to a time when my piano, song, and dance were my companions. Were these real memories? Did Mama even exist? Who am I?

Was it a real memory when I danced alone in my room after a beating from Mama? As I gently tippy-toed the moves like a ballerina in fear, Mama would hear me.

* * *

I had to start thinking smarter. My memories tell me I have a talent, a song, a dance, and a skill to play the piano. I could start by singing a familiar song.

"My eyes are weak and heat to fleet, dust or riches will I meet." I sang to no end.

And even though this was probably the most sorrowful song you've heard, it comforted me—a comfort in knowing that there is something real.

Something that I could hold on to. But this was Chicago, and what would I do to survive? A moan rose from within.

* * *

Well, at least that's still the same.

"But for now, I'm in Chi-Town. Get used to it

bitches." I whispered while lying in the alley.

Chapter Six: The Streets of Chicago

The following morning, despite being homeless and having an amnesiac mental case, I felt a glimmer of hope. A mysterious figure caught my eye, but I hesitated, fearing potential danger.

When I finally glanced over, the person looked away. Each time I turned back, the person evaded my gaze. "Strange," I thought, "this cat-and-mouse game."

From what I could tell, the figure appeared to be girl-like but shabby. I decided to approach this enigmatic individual.

"Hey, who are you?" I called out, peering and waving in her direction. She ran away, and I without thinking pursued.

"Dang, you're fast. Stop running. I won't hurt you," I gasped. Suddenly, she halted and gazed back at me. To my astonishment, it was a younger version of myself!

She looked like she had been through tough times, just like me.

Despite feeling unsettled by encountering this version of myself, I found a strange sense of comfort in the idea that conversing with her might bring to light on all the bizarre events of the past few days — I mean year.

I was unnerved by this vision of my former self – a small, gaunt figure staring back at me with familiar eyes that I had long forgotten were so beautiful.

No wonder Mama was always so envious.

This younger version scared me a bit. It didn't seem right that she just appeared out of nowhere. Was she stalking me this whole time?

She looked so hungry. I knew that look and had to help. I hope she ain't a killer like me. God help me.

"Are you hungry?" I questioned. She nodded, and I offered her my last piece of bread.

The cashier from the bakery thoughtfully snuck this piece of bread when I wasn't looking.

But now, this little girl version of me quickly grabbed my bread and devoured it before I could say a word to stop her.

I don't think she bothered to chew. Her face was puffy, and a slight smile emerged from her sad demeanor.

"Be careful, girl, you gonna choke," I said like a Mama that I wish I had.

She was something I needed — someone in worse shape than me who I could take care of.

But how am I supposed to take care of this child? I can barely take care of myself. What could I do?

How could I validate these events as

accurate? Is this girl who is me—this girl who I can see through my eyes—who hurts as I hurt?

What am I to believe in this unfamiliar reality? I wiped my eyes and looked upon the city, and it was immense.

This terrified me because Chicago is a sprawling metropolis that dwarfed my perceived hometown of Baton Rouge, Louisianna.

The streets teemed with life—business people rushing to work, tourists marveling at the skyscrapers, street performers entertaining crowds, and the countless souls who, like me, were trying to survive.

I looked once more at a puddle of water. I was a ghost of my former self and most certainly unrecognizable to anyone who might have known me a year ago.

My once-bright eyes were now shadowed with fatigue and fear. I had learned to navigate the harsh realities of the streets, find temporary refuge in shelters or abandoned buildings, and always be on the lookout for danger.

How else could I have survived so long? And this little girl? Wait, where did she go? Maybe she was a figment of my imagination.

Shit, that figment took my last piece of bread! I looked in panic because my stomach was growling again. Finally, I noticed the half-eaten bread just ahead of my line of sight.

As I ate, I noticed again that the day was turning to night. I had been pondering and imagining all day with no hope in sight.

"GOD HELP ME!" I screamed. "I can't do this anymore."

So, instantly, I ran from this desolate alley to the ongoing traffic with a full burst of speed. I had to end this madness now.

The last thing I remember was the loud screeching noises from oncoming traffic.

Someone had pulled me from the traffic and intervened on what was my end—the end of my story, to be exact. I found myself surrounded by many people asking if I was okay.

A woman of African descent held my face. "What is your name, child? My name is Olivia, she then said.

Another woman screamed in the distance, "OH GOD, SOMEONE GET AN AMBULANCE!"

I sat there on the sidewalk, surrounded by strangers.

As I wiped my tears her tears, I tried to stand, but this woman, Olivia, would not let me.

"Do not move. You've been and need medical attention. At least let someone look you over," Olivia begged me.

I nodded in agreement and stayed sitting on the concrete. As we waited for the ambulance to arrive, Olivia grabbed my head. I felt slightly weak all of a sudden and out of breath.

I could see the different faces, the same unfamiliar faces beyond Olivia. The crowd looked as though they had seen a miracle.

"Am I dying" I asked Olivia. My thoughts moved slower as one beat, and I felt my body slipping away.

"Stay with me, child," Olivia said

But I couldn't. My life seemed to be slipping away.

I began to close my eyes, and nothing but light surrounded me. Then, a great darkness overcame this light. The light was small, and the darkness enveloped me.

I was light surrounded by darkness. I held my hand in front of my face, or what I believed to be a face, and it was light.

Then the light was gone, and I was completely enveloped by darkness. I could see nothing or hear nothing. I was alone—but not cold, hungry, or wanting anything—just alone.

Then my eyes slowly opened, and a bright ceiling lit directly in my sight, causing me to squint. Someone said. Dim the light she's awake. I looked over, and this stranger, Olivia, was at my bedside.

"Who are you?" I whispered in a faint

voice.

"My name is Olivia. I wanted to make sure you were okay. I'd never seen anything like that before, but I have heard of such occurrences in my home village," Olivia said.

"Wait, please, I just need to rest," I whispered.

I closed my eyes for a moment, but Olivia persisted.

"I'm sorry, but I can be very direct. I must tell you this if you can listen." Olivia said.

'Okay, but I can't promise I will stay up for your story." I said.

"I understand," Olivia said.

"When I was a girl in Ghana, 12 years to be exact, I had a friend possessed by the Adze. I witnessed as she tried to end her life by jumping off of a roof.

Strangely, I saw her jump and fall to the ground. Expecting her to die, but she didn't. She was hurt as you are but not dead." Olivia said.

"I witnessed you jump before a bus and thrust past several moving vehicles. I saw one run over you. Yet you live." Olivia said.

I believed every word she said, and even though it was utterly incomprehensible, it made all the sense in the world. But I couldn't speak much. All I could murmur was, "My name is Celeste."

Olivia continued to reveal what she knew of this ancient creature that possessed me, the Adze. This creature was not exactly as described in Western African civilization folklore.

It usually preyed on children and possessed them either through a spell invoked by a witch or a need for self-preservation.

Unlike the Western African stories, in some cases, the Adze Olivia spoke about needing to latch on to a child—but not just any child, a child of light or a good child, as they would say here in America.

But much more than Americans would associate with a good child. A child of light had unique

113

abilities and was destined to do something remarkable to help this world.

It loved to destroy that goodness that was within.

The Adze traveled into the child as a firefly or an ethereal light. It also could shape-shift the child's appearance primarily and, if threatened, into something more terrifying.

Olivia didn't want to talk too much about what the animal was that the Adze transformed into.

I believe her friend transformed, and it was too difficult for her to speak of. Olivia continued to explain that she was in danger, as was I. The Adze is also vampiric and will eventually consume me from within.

I was thirsty and asked Olivia if she could get me something. Olivia begrudgingly agreed but seemed hellbent on continuing this story. She told me she would ask the nurse to bring some water for me.

My head still hurt some, and I held it to hold the pain at ease. But it was to no avail; the pain just increased.

My hands were thin, and I wondered if another time slippage had occurred while in the hospital. The thinness of my arms was horrific.

My bones nearly showed that they had protruded, similar to someone with extreme food deficiencies.

I looked on as Olivia left my hospital bed and room. Olivia, a woman of African descent, had a thin frame and light skin.

Her features were deep African features, and her eyes were fierce. But she seemed like there was something bothering her.

Mama was evil, and although before I wasn't sure she even existed and felt she was a result of my fractured mind, Mama deserved everything and anything coming to her.

Mr. Resler did not deserve the backlash of this Adze if that is indeed what I am. But how could I reconcile these thoughts to clarity? How could I return to a sanity that was deserving of me?

As I pondered the events of my life and this moment, my heart sank. The weight of it all is ensuring my recovery. My plight may be death or something else, but I must try to hang on for fear that this beast within will consume me and be let loose on the world.

Another thought occurred to me as I noticed a mirror on the side table next to me. I reached and looked at the reflection.

I was receiving oxygen through my nostrils and was hooked up to every medical device imaginable. The person in the mirror was completely unfamiliar to me.

My face looked not just malnourished;

my features had changed drastically.

If anyone were looking for me, they would have no luck. There's no way to pin any crime, Mr. Resler or Mama, on me because the person I was did not exist anymore.

Chapter Seven: Phantom of Hope

Olivia was still away as I looked at the ceiling and closed my eyes. I didn't know what to expect.

Who else had witnessed what Olivia saw? According to her theory, the Adze was a part of me. But was she mad as well?

According to Olivia, I had survived multiple impacts with vehicles.

I couldn't think of these things anymore. So, I closed my eyes and imagined myself in Paris with a Mama who loved me.

My imagination could instantly take me to places like that, and everything would be better, if only for a moment.

But this time, I had no imagination. My mind was not at peace but filled with something quite dark. When I closed my eyes, that place of darkness appeared. It terrified me—not because of the darkness but because I felt at home there.

In this darkness, my mind was too quiet. It was peaceful, with nothing in the background—no birds or animals, no wind or whistling of the wind, no white noise—not even the noise you hear when it is quiet.

The noise is faint or hollow. Not even that white noise. The quiet was as if someone had turned off all sound, and not even my breath was heard in this dark place.

I could see in this place but had no hands. I could move but had no feet. And, of course, I could hear what I thought was a form of thought without words, just knowing what was and what was to be.

In this place, I did not know myself or know of anything that existed or care of it. My cares were of nothing and another purpose. The purpose is to be who I am.

But what was this Adze oer was I as I know — the girl who lived with a deranged supposed Mama and escaped barely with her life. Only to travel from Baton Rouge, Louisiana, to Chicago. Not to mention living on the streets for a year.

I had to keep my eyes open as long as

possible because of fear. Otherwise, I would drift away to this other state of existence. If I thought of the tune and piano playing I loved so dearly, that could keep me awake.

I began to sing a sorrowful tune: "My eyes are weak and heat to fleet, dust or riches will I meet." I sang to my heart's content, and then I felt happy until a voice joined me in singing—a voice like mine but a younger, lighter version.

I stopped singing and held my chest for a moment. I sang a little, and then the voice sang a little. I hummed some, and the voice followed. The voice mimicked me, just like the little girl in the alley.

The girl was me. Could anyone hear this

madness? Or was this in my mind? I stopped once more, taking a deep breath. Then I heard a deep breath taken. Shit! Can I even breathe?

"Shit! Can I even breathe?" The voice said.

"Look, whoever you are. Please, you are scaring the shit out of me." I said.

I was holding onto the edge of my hospital bed. I looked around. I listened, and there was no response. This may be in my imagination.

Olivia finally enters my hospital room with water. And not a minute too soon. I drank in small sips for fear of choking. As the water rushed down my throat, it almost felt like I could drown.

I hadn't felt this way since I was a little girl. One day, Mama—the woman who said she was my Mama—took me on a trip. I couldn't have been more than 4 or 5 years old. I remember because it was before I had to go to school with kids.

This was when I was home with Mama all the time. I don't know how Mama made money, but she didn't work a regular 9 to 5. She seemed to be always home. I guess whatever she did to earn a living, it was when I went to sleep.

I sipped once more and continued thinking about the trip Mama took me on when I was five. Mama said I would learn a lot that day, and I indeed did.

We finally arrived at our destination, the lake I mentioned. It was a pretty lake. Mama was all smiles; I couldn't figure out why she was smiling so much.

When we arrived, I asked her how we had come to this lake, Mama. Was it to watch the birds catch the fish?

Mama grinned like a Cheshire cat. She said, "Oh no, we're here to learn, remember." Then she smiled, but her smile turned into a different look.

"Let's walk towards the pier's edge, sweetie," Mama said.

I thought this was strange, even as a child, because Mama was very stern with me and never called me sweetie.   Mama looked away for a moment as her voice changed.

"I've always had a hard life; it just got harder with you. So, you are either gonna get stronger, or you will not make it. I can't carry dead weight anymore."

At this point, Mama was holding her hands and rubbing them erratically. In a very instant moment, Mama grabbed my hand and yanked me - more like dragging me to the edge of the pier.

Well, it was more like dragging me because, at this point, I began to sense something was

very wrong. Mama thrust me into the lake water. All I
could think of was my inevitable death.

As I sank to my imminent death,
something in me came alive. My legs and arms seemed
to move on their own, and although I had little
experience in swimming, my body could swim.

As I moved to the pier from which Mama
had thrown me, the water seemed part of me. I could
pull myself up only to realize Mama was sitting in the
car watching me from afar.

Mama just looked as I walked back
drenched.

I'm not sure why this memory entered
my mind, but my forehead began to sweat at this

moment. The nurses came in quickly, and Olivia hit the button on my remote to call them.

As the nurses attended to me, I could hear Olivia saying something but couldn't make it all out. My eyes rolled back, and I faded into unconsciousness.

"You had a seizure, but the nurses say you are stabilized," whispered Olivia as my eyes gently opened.

I looked at Olivia and tried to speak, but the words came out as if they were whispered.

"Why are you helping me?" I whispered. It took everything out of me to speak.

"You remind me of my friend. Not only is the fact of the scenario very much a Deja Vu for me, but you favor her, which is uncanny.

And these events happened 20 years ago, so you could not be her." Olivia said.

I looked at this woman, Olivia, trying to comprehend what she said and what this could mean.

"Please, explain more," I said.

Olivia looked at me and explained that just being in the presence of the Adze could be dangerous and that she may anger the entity.

She explained that this could not be a coincidence and felt strange and unsettling.

I looked at the clock, and it was just 6:00 p.m., but it felt like I had been there for days or months.

I managed to ask her a question.

"How long have I been here in the hospital?" I asked.

"Just for today. Why does it feel longer? Oliva asked.

I nodded in agreement as Olivia looked at me in terror.

"Are you ready to listen?" Olivia asked hesitantly.

I replied yes in a whisper. But I was apprehensive. I was faking my strength on the outside and terrified on the inside.

Mama would've slapped me by now for

being so weak. Mama would say something mean like 'Bitch, make me a sandwich and stop all this nonsense."

Shit, I am starting to get sidetracked. I was doing so well with that until now.

"Are you okay?" Olivia asked with a concerned look on her face.

I nodded in agreement.

"It's just that you looked like you were somewhere else for a moment," Olivia said with a concerned look.

"I'm fine," I whispered.

Olivia looked cautiously as though I were some caged animal that would cause her harm.

"Before I begin the story of the Adze, I want you to know that you are in danger. Everything in me tells me the Adze has you." Olivia said.

"Just tell the fucking story and stop stringing me ALONG!" I blurted out.

I held my mouth in confusion, not knowing why I would say something like that to this otherwise very kind woman. This was something Mama would say.

I was so embarrassed and ashamed. Had I become a monster just like Mama?

Olivia stepped back but looked at me sympathetically, more like a cager trying to assess whether this was worth caging this wild beast.

"I'm not a monster - I'm sorry!" I said, sobbing.

Olivia rushed to me and held me tight. Just like a Mama or sibling would.

"Okay, let's start over, okay," Olivia said with a cautious yet stern look.

I nodded, and she began to tell me about the Adze.

Chapter Eight: Phantom of Hope Revelations

Olivia started to recount the events that led her to the Adze. "I told you about when I was a 12-year-old girl in Ghana.

I had a friend the Adze possessed. This friend was my little sister, who was just seven years old. I witnessed her attempting to end her life by jumping off a roof.

It was strange because I saw her jump and fall to the ground. I expected her to die, but she was hurt, not dead.

But I didn't fully explain what life was like before that. When I was young, there were many stories of various boogeymen to scare the children into doing what they were supposed to do.

Of all the boogeymen, only one terrified us, including the adults. The adults told stories of the Adze with deep concern and fear, not playfulness.

The adults would gather us children before the moon was full and forbid us from staying out late or disobeying.

They would say that if you stayed out too late, especially if you wandered away from the village and went to the lake, the Adze would take you to another realm, and you would never return the same.

The adults said that if you screamed, no one would hear you; if you tried to run, the Adze would outrun you. If you fought, you might anger the Adze; things are worse than death.

My father would look at me sternly because he knew I loved the water and swimming, especially at night. My sister Cassea also enjoyed the night and swimming; she was very naughty and did not listen to our parents.

One night, my father pulled me aside during the stories and told me something I would never forget. He said he had seen the Adze and that it was as real as you and me.

My father then did something I had never seen him do; he wept before me and made me promise not to go to the lake under any circumstances.

He knew Cassea, and I loved to swim even when we were told not to. The ancestors protected the village, but the lake was not protected outside the town.

So no one hunted that far out at night, and no one owned farmlands that far out, and no one fished either, at least not at night. Seeing my father cry made me cry, and I promised to obey him.

We were three nights away from the full moon. For some reason, the Adze was more active during the full moon. Legend says it's not like the American werewolf lore but something about how the earth is aligned.

You see, the Adze is an entity that exists in space, and some say outside of time in some instances. My father told me that when he saw the Adze, he couldn't explain it, but it was terrifying to him.

He said he was little but remembered an elder pulling him toward the village border. He had wandered off as a boy and got too far.

The Adze looked at my father, who said it looked straight into his soul. My father was paralyzed for a week and could not speak for a month.

As story time continued, we learned more about the Adze. Its playful nature attracted children in particular. The elders said that the Adze was almost awkward yet profound simultaneously.

I moved differently than we did, not in a good way either.

As I looked at Baba during the story, he

nodded and gave me a look that meant I should pay close attention. So I nodded back and continued to listen.

Cassea didn't seem as interested. I felt I needed to tell her what my father said and made a special note to do so after storytime.

But Cassea had disappeared. She was gone, and I was the only one aware. Baba was looking closely, and I couldn't escape his gaze. So, I had to find a way to distract him so I could look for her.

I asked the elders to make Baba's favorite alcoholic drink. Baba was pleased and thankful for my thoughtfulness.

I've always remembered that this drink

made Baba sleepy and want to talk with Mama privately. At the time, I didn't know what speaking in private meant.

But now, as an adult, I know it was a sexual stimulant for him, and Mama didn't seem to mind one bit.

After finishing his drink, Baba encouraged me to continue listening to Adze's stories and come home immediately after story time with my older cousins.

I nodded and hugged Baba tightly as though it was the last time I would see him. In truth, I was unsure if I would come back. If I were to venture past the village border looking for Cassea, then this might mean my inevitable death.

But I didn't want to leave her alone, even though her actions were foolish and selfish. I didn't want my friend to die.

So, I also slipped away and ran deep into the woods and then to the lake at the border of my village. There, she was waving. I thought she was crazy.

She had a bathing suit on and was ready to jump in the lake for a swim.

I yelled, "Cassea, don't jump in the lake, come back!". But she jumped in anyway. I looked for any sign after she jumped in, but the lake was still as though no one inhabited or occupied it.

My heart began to race, and I ran towards

the lake.

Cassea suddenly emerged from the lake with a calm but disturbing look. I asked her if she was okay and if it was time to return to the village before the Adze found us.

She looked at me dumbfounded for a moment as if what I said required more thought process on her part. Then Cassea said something. She said, 'Why are you so afraid of me?

I would never hurt you, not unless you tried to harm me.'

I looked at Cassea closely; this was not the goofy and playful friend I knew. Instead, she was intentional with her movements and words.

I stepped back cautiously, but she reassured me I was safe.

I asked if you are the Adze, why, my friend, and what you want with us. Why are you terrorizing my village, my people, my family & friends?

Adze, talking through my friend, made its case to me. Not that it had to. However, due to my deep connection to Cassea, it wanted to answer my questions.

"This one is very disobedient, and I prefer obedient children," said the Adze.

I was terrified that the Adze was speaking to me. But it did not look through my soul like Baba said it would. Instead, it looked compassionately to me.

I was now confused because Baba had

mentioned how terrifying the Adze was, but it was not in my case. Could it have been testing me?

I sat calmly and looked for a while, not saying anything. The Adze did the same. It mimicked me while possessing Cassea.

"Cassea, are you in there?" I said.

But there was no response, just a blank stare.

What was I supposed to do?

I beckoned Cassea to return to the village, but her look began to change. I told her I was scared and needed to return immediately.

She looked at me. I took a deep breath

and turned to run until her hand on my shoulder stopped me.

"Wait, don't leave me," Cassea said.

Cassea was now directly speaking and pleading with me.

She explained that the Adze was misunderstood and that I should stay with them.

She said they would take care of me and not to be afraid.

But I was afraid. Very afraid. I nodded in agreement.

Cassea spoke softly but at a level, I could hear clearly in her voice. She was confident and reassured in her delivery of this recount. She explained that the Adze is dangerous and that care should be taken when approaching it.

Cassea told me the Adze is a part of her spirituality, and although we believe it is folklore from the Ifa spiritual system, it falls under war.

In the Yoruba religion, Ifa is the main deity. Many deities are worshiped, and these dairies are known as Orishas. These Orishas represent various forces of nature, including life, love, war, fertility, and the sea.

Cassea repeated that Adze opposes the war deity in your culture.

The Adze then began to speak softly and

playfully. The deity of war angers me. You call this deity Ogun. I am a malevolent spirit. I am a type Ogun. I bring misfortune, illness, and death.

Do not bother taking this child, Cassea, to a Balalawo (Ifa priest). There will be no need for a divination session.

You may try to prescribe specific rituals, sacrifices, or offerings to appease me, but it will not work in this case. Cassea is mine, and I am hers. We are twin flames.

Your tribe is of Ewe people of Ghana and consistently refer to me as the Adze. While correct in a sense, I am more than that and am more in line with the Yoruba religion.

Has your Baba told you anything about the Yoruba religion? Did he tell you we met before when he was a boy?

Did he tell you your family left Nigeria shortly after encountering me? Did he tell you what the Ifa priest attempted to do to me? They know nothing of me.

Did he of your people the Ewe? You are a perplexed person. You don't even know which God is God.

I couldn't believe Cassea; this entity spoke like an adult from a child's tongue.

"You cannot leave us; we adore you. You have my favor, and we shall cause much destruction, and Chaos and Cassea will know nothing of it. She will be completely blind to what is occurring. " Said the Adze

I asked Adze to please let my sister go and take me instead. I pleaded that she was too young, but Adze just laughed menacingly. I took a breath and pleaded for my sister's life.

The Adze paused and looked at me. It said it would spare what I believed to be her life under one condition. I had to kill my sister.

The Adze said we could return to the village, and Cassea would know nothing of what occurred.

But this was a trick, for the Adze was a

trickster at heart and played me for a fool.

I agreed, and my sister and I returned to the village unbeknownst to anyone.

The next few days leading up to her almost fatal jump were ups and downs. One moment, everything was fine, and I could talk to my little sister and teach her things.

The next moment, she had turned for worse to the Adze.

The last day I remember my sister was when we went to the market with Baba. I had almost forgotten she was possessed. The whole day was typical.

She was herself, and I just enjoyed her. Then, when we passed by the mangos, my sister Cassea stole one and ran straight across the street to a building.

I ran after her, and Baba ran after me. Cassea ran up the stairs to the top of the building and to the roof. She was running so fast that I could barely keep up with her.

When I finally caught up with her, Cassea was smiling, and I knew this was the Adze taunting me. The Adze said to me that it was time and that I would have to push Cassea off the roof to her death.

But I couldn't hold up my end of the bargain, greatly angered the Adze.

"Then you will not see your sister for many moons. I will cause great torment in her life, and you will not be able to do anything about it," said the

Adze.

Then she jumped off the roof and fell to the ground. It looked like her body was warped as she rose from the fall.

Cassea looked up at me, and I knew it was my sister with a sad look; then, she ran. Baba and Mother were devastated.

We never found my sister Cassea.

Chapter Nine: What a Predicament?

My sister and I had a song we sang together. Do you sing Celeste?

I could barely fathom all that this woman Olivia had just told me of the tragic events that led to her sister's disappearance.

Olivia looked away and began sobbing. I could barely move at this point due to an extreme onset of exhaustion. My body felt so weak, and each breath was belabored. Each movement was also very labor intensive.

My days will come to an end. I'm so weak. What if this whole thing is some delusion? I thought this was a very elaborate delusion.

Olivia wept so much I thought she was

going to die of grief right there at the foot of my hospital bed.

I managed to muster up some strength and said, "I find it quite puzzling that you talk of this, Adze, you say?"

Then I waved to Olivia and closed my eyes for just a moment.

"Can you hear me?" Olivia said.

"I must have dozed off," I said. My eyes focused, and Olivia was looking at me. "I must be in terrible shape for a stranger to pity me," I said.

Have you ever dozed off and felt like an eternity had elapsed? Well, this is how it felt—not just

30 minutes or an hour, but an eternity.

After a little more time had passed, my voice felt better, and my strength had returned. But then, as I looked at Olivia crying, something felt left out.

I couldn't explain it, but I believed this woman was hiding something from me. I couldn't explain it, but - "Oh my stomach, it hurts." My stomach made a loud growl, followed by immense pain.

"How can you sit here with a straight face after losing your sister? After telling that story?" I said to Olivia.

Olivia jumped back and cautiously watched me, not saying a word. She stood frozen, not seemingly breathing.

Wait a minute, can you see this? She is not movin'. What time is it? I looked at the clock on the wall, and the second hand was not moving.

I got off my bed, dressed in the patient garment, and held the back part. I never understood why they didn't make these hospital gowns with a button at least to close the back portion if needed.

I looked, walked past Olivia's frozen frame, and peeped out the door. Well, hell, everybody was frozen. I walked past nurses, patients, and doctors. I even put my finger up someone's nose to see what would happen.

Nothing happened for a while, and things started changing around me. Everything went black, and

I was alone. There were no nurses, doctors, secretaries, or patients—and then not even me. I couldn't sense who I was anymore.

There was nothing but void. It seemed like a familiar void, but an unnerving one at that.

My skin began to rip apart. I screamed in agony, "HELP ME, SOMEONE STOP THIS !" my flesh and bones were torn to pieces, and I was nothing.

As hard as I could, I tried to grasp a thought. Any thought. But I didn't even know what thought was, just that there was something to learn; I was nothing, and it was familiar.

There was another in this void. Another lost nothing like myself, but It felt like this nothing was more than just nothing. Perhaps it was nothing and nothing to make me or something. It felt as though my existence was all that was left of me.

Then, out of somewhere that was nowhere came groans. A familiar groan, but not just of fear, anger, hate, jealousy, strife, destructiveness, pain, and mania, and opt not of this realm.

I became more and more within this feeling. It consumed me, making me happy to be consumed by it. Nothing made me happier but to destroy and cause conflict. For somehow, I felt wronged. Revenge is my song, and jealousy is my lover.

But what or who could have wronged me? As my thoughts flowed in the void, I began to realize that the nothing was something, the other something.

My words did not form correctly, and I could not express what was what. Or who was it, and why was it there? Not far but near, not unfriendly but my only friend.

I tried and tried to remember, but nothing came easy, and this seemed like an impossible task. So I stopped trying and stayed in the nothingness, Hoping my other nothing would come to me.

Nothing happened, and nothing passed. And then something passed, and I knew it was time. Then I heard a voice, a very familiar voice. It was the little girl from the alley; the voice mimicked me.

But the voice was not the same. It was more cautionary. The voice began to tell me to be wary of strangers who come as friends. The voice wanted me to remember.

The voice was dangerous, but not to me. The voice explained a feeling of sorrow. The voice was mischievous and vengeful and full of anger and hate, but not to me; it said to another who is full of deceit.

The voice came closer until it looked at me from the inside to the outside realm.

I was filled with rage and anger. Something very, very underhanded had occurred. I became bitter and did not know why.

The voice became primarily a feeling,

and the feeling told us to destroy those who wronged us. But who could wrong us?

My eyes began to open as Olivia stood in the corner, not crying but still looking cautiously at me. Why was she so concerned with me?

Did I do something to her? "Who are you? YOU CLAIM TO BE SOMEONE I KNOW, BUT WHO ARE YOU." My voice thundered as this question was asked to Olivia.

Olivia backed away and said, "This was a mistake; I should leave." But I would not let her; she could not leave without telling me the truth.

My stomach began to groan. Olivia looked terrified at this time and began to plead with me

to release her. But I did not. I moved closer to her
without moving. I held her without holding. And I began
to pull the skin from her finger.

"Tell me the truth, Olivia," I said.

"Help! Someone help me. She's going to
kill me." Said Olivia. "I should have killed you when
you were a child," said Olivia.

I stopped and looked. "What did you
say?"

"You heard me; I should have killed you!
I should have killed you!" Said Olivia.

"You mean to tell me I'm your little
sister? IMPOSSIBLE!" I said.

"No bitch, very possible," Olivia said in an American tone.

"And you not from Africa either," I said.

"No, I made all the shit up," said Olivia.

"Bitch, I hate you!" said Olivia in a devious tone.

"You made all of this up! Is Mama even real?" I said under my breath.

"And, yes, you did have an evil Mama. Don't you remember? You ate her!" said Olivia. You some kind of a beast. Maybe werewolf, but not like in the movies or on TV."

"All I know is, you need to let me go

before the full moon tonight." said Olivia.

I stood there trying to process what she just said.

"Bitch, can you snap out of your daydreaming spells and unfreeze time so that I can get some medical attention." Said Olivia.

"I won't let you go until you tell me who I am. Are you even my sister?" I said.

Olivia was squirming in my clutches like a prey, and I was the hunter. She was lying even now that her life was in danger. I couldn't trust her. But I had to take a chance.

All I could remember was living with Mama. I couldn't remember Olivia at all. It was just

Mama and me. But this rage and anger within me is so intense. Maybe what she is saying is true.

"I've been following you for months now," Olivia said. Her hand was profusely dripping with blood. She was holding her hand tight while trying to stay balanced.

"We're from Chicago and don't live far from this hospital," Olivia said.

"But what about Baton Rouge, Louisiana? I just came here to Chicago!" I said.

Olivia explained, "Bitch, Louisiana was where Mama's people were from. We went there on holiday, but we didn't live there." She said.

"Everything you remember is an illusion,

just like the story about us in Africa. I just did a little

research in the library about African folklore and

meshed things together to create a version of the entity

Adze.

It's supposed to be some mythical

creature from the mythology of the Ewe people in West

Africa." Olivia said.

"So what about Mr. Resler and Ms.

Claudine? Did I kill or eat them too?" I said.

"You killed and have eaten a lot of

people. I don't know who those people are." Olivia said.

Then Olivia began to plead with me. Not

for her life but to destroy myself. She said that was the

only way to end all this. And that I was psychotic and

deranged.

Olivia kept going on and on about the plight of the world and that Mama was wrong, but she didn't deserve to die and certainly not to be eaten.

Olivia had the nerve to say that this evil woman, who told me I was not her daughter, was not that bad.

Olivia continued on and on about how more time had passed than I thought. But for some reason, I had only aged a year.

I was confused on this one because Olivia looked like she was in her late twenties.

She kept going on and on. And to be completely honest, it started to annoy me. My stomach began to moan quite a bit.

Have you ever been so hungry that you could eat a horse? Well, I was. I guess Olivia could see how unconcerned I was. She now seemed terrified as I stopped her storytelling.

After all, this is my story, not hers!

"If you can concentrate long enough before passing out, I have just two questions. Your answer will determine your fate, and I guess everyone else's if what you say is true." I said.

Olivia nodded, now looking very pale yet somewhat appetizing. Oh, shit, she is right. But how come I can't remember anything?

Here are my questions to Olivia. The first

was an easy one. I asked her, "If you are my sister, my real sister. Then why didn't you protect me from Mama?"

Mama was so cruel, and I couldn't imagine a sibling, especially an older sibling, not protecting the younger one.

Olivia looked dumbfounded. So, do you need me to repeat myself? She said no, I heard you. "So speak then," I said.

Olivia cleared her throat. I knew she was getting ready to go through another chapter-long story. Here we go again. Look, make this quick. I'm hungry, my voice thundered, followed by an undertoned groan.

"But, to answer your question, I hated

you. And Mama did, too. Mama adopted you, and all sorts of strange things happened in our family. It took a while to figure out. But eventually, we put things together that the source was you." Olivia said.

"Look, I'm sorry what happened to you. Suppose you could just let me go. I won't bother you. I'll disappear." Olivia said.

"Okay, so you all wanted to kill me since I was a baby. Now, you've raised my curiosity. I'll add a bonus question. So, did you figure out how to kill me?" I said.

Olivia motioned and said no, she didn't know of a way to kill me, and that stuff is fairytale, silver bullets and such.

I still didn't believe her, but something inside me kept urging me to get more out of Olivia. I was so hungry.

Why would she put her life in danger to ask me to destroy myself? What was her real motif in connecting with me?

So that's what I asked for the last question before massacring Olivia. She screamed so loudly that I thought the nurses would come on in. I devoured every limb of Olivia, every part, ending with the heart.

What was she thinking?

Chapter Ten: What a Calamity

As I sat on the floor just thinking.
Something was not right. There was not a drop of blood
on the floor, and it looked so clean—just a little too
clean.

I looked around, and my bed was made
up like no one had slept there. This was a little strange.
But maybe I'm just a very precise and clean whatever I
am.

But this was odd considering I was in bed
for such a long time and even odder that no blood or any
remnants of Olivia remained. Not even a finger.

I wonder what she meant by more time
had passed than I had realized. Just like Mr. Resler, I
had failed to question her enough. What year is it for

real, and how old should I be?

I looked out the window, and it was still dark. A slight panic arose, and I wondered when I would need to eat again? Olivia and Mama were easy kills because of their evil nature. But how would or could I kill innocent people?

And why has no one entered since the nurses assisted me?

Panic continued to rise within me, and then I heard what I knew would come sooner or later. My twin person giggled from somewhere. I thought this little girl had to be in here somewhere. Where could she be?

I searched everywhere in the room except

one place: under the bed. Then, as I slowly looked there, she was smiling in the darkness of the center of the bed. I motioned for her to come out. And she did.

I then motioned for her to sit on the bed with me, and she did. Looking at her, I couldn't help but notice her face. There was dried blood all over her face.

I wiped some of the dry mixed with wet blood off her face, then tasted it. Yep, that's Olivia, all right. I asked her if she was me and I was her. She smiled but said nothing.

No repeating or anything, just a smile. But I didn't know what to make of it. She would've killed me or tried to kill me a long time ago. I'm sure there were many opportunities.

I asked her to stay on the bed while I looked in the mirror. Something was bugging me ever since we met in the alley. So, I needed to double-check to make sure this was real.

I went to the mirror, and my face was bloody, not dry, but fresh blood. I washed my face off for appearances and couldn't just walk outside in public like this.

My face was clean, not a scratch or blemish. I motioned for my younger self to come and clean her face, and she did. She looked just like me and smiled.

But something was still not right. Olivia had mentioned that a lot of time had passed. And as I was devouring her something, she managed to gurgle something through her bloody throat.

What was it she said?

I remember now. Olivia gurgled, and both of you must die in her last plea. But I was so enraged I didn't realize she was talking about this girl. The frustration of trying to remember who I am was wearing on me.

I should lie in bed, just in case nurses come by. But what will I do with this young girl? She looks like she's seven years old now.

I can't remember her age before, but she looked like seven. For whatever reason, I didn't fear her.

But wanted to protect this girl. Although I had no blemishes, I looked older than sixteen or seventeen. My best guess would be my late twenties, like twenty-eight. You see where I'm going with this, don't you?

Exactly this little girl could pass as my daughter. Shit, for all I know, she is my daughter. So that's what I told her. I told her to come in the bed and lay next to me, and when the nurses come in, call me Mama.

"On second thought, you just call me mother," I said. Then, things started to make some sense. This child had to be mine, and Mama hit me in the head so much my memory kept lapsing.

But after I fed on Olivia, my mind seemed slightly better.

Then, in an instant, the memories began to come flooding back. The labor of my first child and Mama and Olivia destroying him.

Then, I gave birth to this one whom I had in secret. Jesse was the father, and he was a good person.

Mama and Olivia killed him foolishly, thinking he was like me. He was just a regular human being. I was eighteen with my first pregnancy and baby boy William from Jesse, and nineteen with this one, I named my second child Amara.

Amara was good at hiding, but Mama found her one day and tried to destroy her, just like

William and Jesse. That's what happened that night. Amara saved me from Mama and has been with me ever since.

I couldn't defend myself because I didn't feed. But I did provide food, mostly dogs like poor old Satchel, for Amara, so she was strong.

Olivia lied. There was a way to kill us, only if we were weak and had fed for a long time.

Both Olivia and Mama wanted me to be as weak as possible before attempting to kill me. Olivia wasn't home and didn't witness Amara feeding on half of Mama's body.

After I saw my baby girl devour half of this woman, my mind went into a shocked state, and I fled. But my baby stayed close, always trying to protect me. She knew my mind was not right, and my heart was broken.

My strong baby girl. Come close to me?

"We've been through a lot, haven't we?" I said to Amara.

She nodded her head and held me tight. We held each other, not wanting to let go. Now that I had all of my faculties. I had to try to explain to Amara how dangerous it is for us.

People will want to destroy us and may or may not discover how to kill us. I continued explaining to Amara that if we were captured, they would separate us.

I continued as Amara listened, but something else was not quite right. It was quiet, and I hadn't heard anything since earlier. No people or anything for that matter.

I told Amara to stay close to me as I slowly uprooted from the bed and walked over to the window. It was still night, and the streetlights were on, but no one was there.

"Amara baby, Mommy is going to change out of these hospital clothes, okay," I said.

I changed into my neatly folded clothes on a chair next to my hospital and put on my sneakers.

Amara and I slowly walked to the door of the hospital room. When I opened it, everyone was

frozen in time. I hadn't thought about this since earlier.
I looked at Amara and asked, "Did you do this, baby?"

But she just looked just as concerned as I.
We continued to exit the hospital. Everything was quiet,
and everyone and everything was frozen.

Somehow, we stepped outside of time
without a way or means to fix it.

So, is this the end of the story for me? Could this
world be doomed? What about the child that is with me,
and how will we navigate this world? A world without
people is a world without time. But what if none of this
was real?

Beep beep beep beep beep beep.

I felt someone touching my cheek, but I could

not make out while there was no one there but myself and my child.

"Celeste, Celeste, Celeste, this is Dr. Melvin." Dr. Melvin said.

"Your psychosis has become very advanced, and we here at Mercy Hospital want to help you. Can you hear me, Celeste? Can you hear me?" Dr. Melvin said.

My eyes could barely open as I whispered.

"I don't know who I am. I don't know who I am."

Please help me.